The Christmas Giver

Corena Elmer

To order additional copies of this book, contact:
Xlibris
844-714-8691
www.Xlibris.com
Orders@Xlibris.com

ISBN: Softcover   978-1-6641-3534-5
         EBook   978-1-6641-3533-8

Print information available on the last page

Rev. date: 12/09/2020

The Christmas Tree

Carrie was a bright young child who was 6 years old and in the first grade.

She also went to a public school and had many friends.

But one of her best friends, Anna, no one could top.

Carrie spent lots of time with Anna, doing things like board games and playing out in the snow.

One day, Carrie came home from school and noticed there were many vans out in the driveway.

She ran in excited and called for her mom.

"Carrie, what do you want Sweetie?"

"Mom, why are all the vans parked outside? I see lots of people, and they're coming into our home with a huge Christmas tree."

"Carrie sweetheart, we're getting ready for Christmas and the people coming in are setting up our home for our big Christmas ball."

Carrie couldn't understand why other people put up their own trees, as a family, when they had tons of people doing all the decorations,

"Mom, I don't understand. Why do we have people doing all our decorations when other families do it together?"

"Oh my sweet little girl, we are very rich and the poor people have to do all the work because they can't afford to hire anyone."

"But Mom, I want to decorate a tree like Anna does."

"Well sweetie, as I say, we are very rich and Anna doesn't even wear nice clothes and comes from a poor family,"

"What does being rich or poor have to do with Christmas Mom?"

"Well, when you have lots of money, you hire people to do things and that saves me time to do other things."

Carrie was still quite confused.

She heard her cell phone beep and it was her best friend Anna.

"Hi, Anna," Carrie said,

"What are we going to do today?"

Carrie was so excited because Anna wanted her to come over and help decorate the tree.

"Mom" Carrie said "can I go over to Anna's?"

"Sure" her mom said, "just be home by dinner time."

"I will Mom, I promise."

Anna quick grabbed her coat and ran to meet Carrie.

She was so full of excitement for her best friend to come over.

"Hi Anna," Carrie yelled. The two girls were holding hands and went over to Anna's small house.

Carrie was confused because her house was so big that she was sure she didn't see all of it, even though she lived there.

Anna was bringing up boxes from downstairs filled with all the Christmas decorations.

Carrie loved the smell of their tiny Christmas tree and was delighted to help decorate this beautiful tree.

So they were off, hanging up lights and putting up beautiful Christmas bulbs.

Anna stood back and looked at their tree, then she asked Carrie what she thought.

"Anna it's beautiful, I wish I could decorate our tree at home, but mom said we hire people to do that for us."

Anna couldn't understand why Carrie's parents didn't put up their own Christmas tree.

Anna's mom came into their little living room and stood back and took a look at the tree.

"Oh my, you girls did a fabulous job, so good that you can have fresh baked cookies that I made."

Anna and Carrie ran to the kitchen and pulled out a chair and sat down.

Anna's mom brought out beautiful cookies that she had baked herself.

Carrie said, "My mom never bakes; we hire people to do that."

Anna's mom wasn't too surprised because she knew Carrie lived on the biggest estate in their whole town, but Anna's mom never judged Carrie's place or how well she lives.

Carrie looked at the clock and it was going on 5:30 p.m. and she know she had to head home.

Anna, I need to go, but before I do, I want you to come over to our Christmas Ball on Christmas Eve."

"Really" Anna said, "but I have no beautiful dresses to wear and my mom can't afford to buy me a fancy dress,"

Carrie giggled, and said "Don't worry I got that all taken care of. But we have to sneak in my room so my mom doesn't see and you can pick out any dress that you want."

"Wow, I can't believe it! Carrie you're my forever best friend."

The girls hugged and Carrie was on her way home.

Carrie ran home and yelled, "Mom I'm home."

"Oh sweet girl, just look at all the present you have under your Christmas tree."

Carrie's eyes just shined when she saw all of those beautiful boxes that were wrapped in bright golden paper with the biggest bows she has ever seen.

"Mom, are those for me?"

"Yes my dear daughter, but there are some under there for your father and I."

"Mom, Anna doesn't have any gifts under her tree. She's my best friend and I can't understand why she has no gifts."

"Oh Carrie, poor people aren't as good as us. We have money and live far better than poor people."

Carrie had tears in her eyes and looked at her mom. "You mean we are better people because we have money?"

"Yes dear. Your dad is a high-paid lawyer and I own my own business, so we are definitely better.

"I guess Anna's mom doesn't work at a high-paying job like your father and I."

Carrie was upset because Anna was her best friend, so Carrie had to think of a way to help Anna get gifts.

Late at night Carrie hid her little wagon on the side of her house. She tiptoed downstairs very quietly.

Carrie looked at their tree and was thinking she was going to help Anna one way or another.

Carrie grabbed a big box and put it in her wagon. Then she went back and grabbed two more.

So she threw her robe on and her boots and went to Anna's house.

Carrie knew that Anna's mom didn't lock the back door, so she pulled her wagon up to the door and slowly opened it. She grabbed one package at a time and gently put the packages under the tree.

Then Carrie stood back and she felt just wonderful for giving her friend her own gifts.

Of course, Carrie pulled the tags off and put Anna's name on it.

Then Carrie tiptoed out of their house and slowly closed the door.

The next morning Anna got up and went downstairs. She saw the tree with gifts under it. She yelled, "Mom, did you put these gifts under the tree? They're so beautiful."

Her mom didn't know what to say, so she finally said, "Honey I didn't do it, I don't know where they came from."

Anna didn't care where they came from she was just excited to see them.

She ate breakfast and called Carrie and told her about the gifts under the tree.

Carrie was so excited that her best friend was happy. And for some reason Carrie felt a beautiful feeling in her heart that she never felt before, but she was totally happy.

Night of the Ball

Christmas Eve, the night of the ball.

Carrie phoned Anna and told Anna to meet her outside so she could sneak her in and let her pick out any fancy dress that she wanted.

Quietly they snuck upstairs to Carrie's room and Anna was so very excited.

"How come your room is so big and you have so many fancy dresses Carrie?"

Carrie said, "I don't know. I guess my mom just loves to shop and buy me dresses."

Anna looked at her closet, which was huge, then she spotted a beautiful dark blue dress with light tiny snowflakes on it.

Carrie said, "Is that the one you want?"

Anna shook her head and said yes and the girls giggled as they got all dressed up to go to the ball.

The two girls went downstairs and there were tons of people there; too many to count.

Anna was so excited, she felt like this was a really good dream.

The girls held hands and danced and danced as their dresses just flowed around them.

All of a sudden the music stopped and the two girls stared at each other. Carrie's mom called out:

"Carrie, is that one of your dresses that Anna has on?"

The whole room was quiet and there were many eyes on them. Carrie said, "Umm, yes Mom, that is one of my dresses."

Carrie's mom was very angry and yelled, "I paid $500 for that dress young lady. Go upstairs to your room and tell that trash Anna she doesn't belong at a ball like this."

Both Carrie and Anna ran upstairs and Carrie handed Anna her backpack. She was very angry at her mom. She helped Anna take off the dress and then she put it in her backpack.

"Take this home Anna; it's yours. I have so many dresses that my mom won't even notice."

Anna gave Carrie a hug and said, "You're the best friend I could ever have."

Carrie had tears in her eyes and walked Anna home.

Christmas Day

Carrie was on a mission. She didn't care what her mom thought of Anna, so early Christmas morning she loaded up her wagon with tons of gifts.

She even went to other neighbors that didn't live in big houses and put a package by their door.

Carrie hid as she watched a small boy open up their door and saw the beautiful package.

Carrie's heart felt like it was growing bigger and she enjoyed this.

She dropped by Anna's house and put more packages under their tree, and even one for Anna's mom.

Then the sun was starting to come up this Christmas day.

She ran upstairs and put her robe on and pretended that she was in bed all night.

Her mom was the first one up and noticed that almost all the gifts were gone. She yelled for her husband and thought they got robbed.

Carrie came down stairs to see what all the yelling was about.

Her mom asked Carrie if she heard anyone last night or seen anyone.

Carrie blinked her eyes and said no.

Carrie's mom asked, "Carrie did you do something to all the gifts under our tree?"

Carrie looked at her mom and said "Yes."

"What did you do, Carrie?"

"I gave the poor people gifts and never felt better."

Her mom looked at her and said "Are you crazy girl? I spent a lot of money on those gifts."

Carrie looked at her mom and all of a sudden there was a very bright light that shown through their window.

Even Carrie's mom was shocked.

As the light glowed on Carrie, she said, "Mom there is nothing wrong with poor people. They're just like us and they struggle. I wanted to help them.

Still Carries mom didn't say anything.

Then Carrie looked at her mom and dad and said "This was the best Christmas that she ever had. For it's better to give than receive, right Dad?"

The End

A special thanks to
my friend Angie,
Who helped me
edit my book.
Your help was greatly
appreciated...

Printed in the United States
By Bookmasters